Past Work, Future Work

Andrew Einspruch

PM Extensions Nonfiction Ruby Level
Caring for Earth
Changing Cultures
Having Fun, Then and Now
Change in the Community
Communities Everywhere
Past Work, Future Work

Rigby PM Extensions Nonfiction
part of the Rigby PM Program
Ruby Level

Published by Harcourt Achieve Inc.
P.O. Box 26015, Austin, Texas 78755.

U.S. edition © 2005 Harcourt Achieve Inc.

First published in 2003 by Cengage Learning Australia
Text © Cengage Learning Australia 2003
Illustrations © Cengage Learning Australia 2003

All rights reserved. No part of the material protected by this copyright may be reproduced or utilized in any form or by any means, in whole or in part, without permission in writing from the copyright owner. Requests for permission should be mailed to: Copyright Permissions, Harcourt Achieve, P.O. Box 26015, Austin, Texas 78755.

Rigby and Steck-Vaughn are trademarks of Harcourt Achieve Inc. registered in the United States of America and/or other jurisdictions.

10 9 8 7 6 5 4 3 2
09

Printed in China by 1010 Printing Limited

Past Work, Future Work
ISBN 0 7578 9237 X

Acknowledgements:
The author and publisher would like to acknowledge permission to reproduce material from the following sources:
AAP Image/AFP, p. 25 top left; Amazon.com, p. 27 bottom; Australian Picture Library/Corbis/Bettmann, pp. 6 top, 16 top and bottom, 18 top and bottom /Schefler Collection, p. 6 bottom /Jim Richardson, p. 9 top /Jim Craigmyle, p. 9 bottom right /Laurent, p. 13/ Richard T. Nowitz, p. 14 top /Franken, p. 14 bottom /John Garrett, p. 15 /Museum of History and Industry, p. 17 bottom /Gunter Marx Photography, p. 26 bottom; Australian War Memorial, p. 23; Digital Stock, p. 4 bottom left; Digital Vision, p. 5 bottom; Newspix, p. 30 bottom; PhotoDisc, pp. 1, 8 top, 9 top and bottom left; PhotoEdit/Michael Newman, pp. 12, 30 top; photolibrary.com/Index Stock, pp. 21 bottom, 28–29 bottom /SuperStock, p. 22 bottom; Stock Photos /Masterfile/Ron Stroud, p. 5 top /John Felingersh, p. 7 bottom /Brian Sytnyk, p. 17 top; Stock Photos, p. 19 bottom left and right /Diana Calder, p. 8 left /Pauline Madden, p. 10 /John Oxley Library, pp. 12 inset, 26 top /Rick Altman, p. 20.

Contents

		Page
Chapter 1	Jobs Come and Go	4
Chapter 2	Why Work?	8
Chapter 3	Life on the Farm	12
Chapter 4	Work Revolution	16
Chapter 5	More Changes	18
Chapter 6	A Job for Life	20
Chapter 7	Women and Work	22
Chapter 8	Information Revolution	24
Chapter 9	The Amazing Disappearing Distance	26
Chapter 10	What will Work Life be Like?	28
	Glossary	32
	Index	Inside back cover

Chapter 1

Jobs come and go

Hop in your time machine and travel back 20 years. When you get there, lean out the window and ask the first person you meet if they could help you find a web designer or a genetic engineer. Be ready for them to give you a blank stare.

Go back another 30 years. Ask someone about working as an astronaut or a computer programmer. Odds are good they'll think you're weird.

Try a bigger jump. Set the dial for the year 1900. Ask someone about being a pilot, a car mechanic, or a film director. More strange looks.

Jobs come. Jobs go. That's the way it has been for hundreds of years.

When no one drives horse-drawn carriages, no one needs a coachman. When everyone has a telephone, there's no need for telegram deliverers. However when someone invents a computer or a jet, we need people to build, fix, sell, and operate them.

A few thousand years ago, choices were pretty limited – hunt, gather, and do whatever was needed to survive.

But that's all different now. **Technology** constantly changes the way we live and the work we do.

Chapter 2

Why Work?

First, let's find out why people work.

Perhaps the answer seems obvious – you work to get money so you can buy things.

Imagine what it used to be like. You (or your family) made all your own clothes, grew your own food, made all your own tools, provided your own entertainment – the list goes on and on.

But not everyone was good at everything. Someone could shoe a horse, but did not like knitting. Or they could heal a wound, but could not tell a decent story.

So people divided up the work to take advantage of the different skills. Along the way, these activities turned into trades, businesses, and jobs.

But don't people work for other reasons?

Work can make you feel useful or helpful. It's a way to contribute to the world. It can let you express yourself (whether you're an artist or a programmer). You can also meet people and learn new things.

Some people choose to work because they enjoy doing what they do.

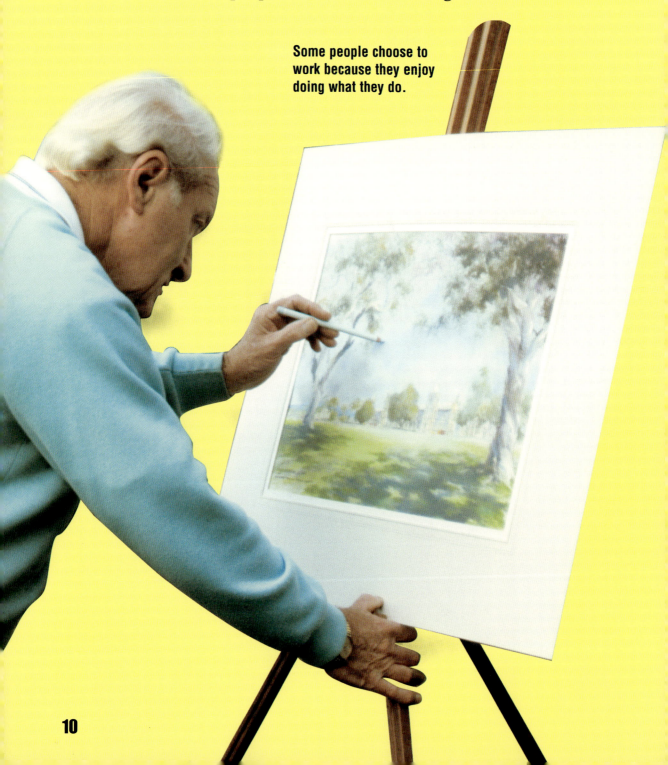

Besides, what would it be like if no one worked? Nothing would ever get done and people would get very bored.

Chapter 3
Life on the Farm

Until around 1700, people spent most of their working lives on two things – food and shelter. Work depended on muscle power more than brainpower. If something needed to be made, it was usually made by hand (or maybe using a simple machine), by someone who lived nearby.

The idea of going to work for someone else to earn a wage had not been invented yet.

Most people simply farmed food or worked in a trade. Leading up to 1700, some manufacturing was done in homes. It was called **cottage industry**, and husband, wife, and children all worked closely together.

A cottage industry today may or may not take place in a home, and may employ workers outside of the family.

Jobs of Old

People's work often became their last name. We still see these surnames today. Think about the origin of surnames like Baker and Tailor. What work do you think people with these names may have done many years ago?

Making candles the traditional way. This man is cutting the ends off these hand-dipped candles.

Here are a few more examples:

A ...	Is someone who...
Cooper	makes barrels
Fletcher	makes arrows
Cartwright	makes wagons
Crocker	makes bowls (crockery)
Chandler	makes candles
Hatcher	raises chickens
Sawyer	saws (a carpenter)

A cooper making oak barrels

Chapter 4

Work Revolution

Mine workers in 1908

The **Industrial Revolution** changed everything. In the 1700s, people began to use steam-powered machines to make things. Machines meant work needed to be done in factories. This was faster and cheaper than cottage industries. Workers became more productive and no longer needed to be skilled in their craft. Prices dropped, so more people could afford to buy more things.

Before the Fair Labor Standards Act in 1938, many children worked the same hours as adults. This young girl is working in a cotton mill in North Carolina.

At the same time, there were big changes in farming. The **Agricultural Revolution** saw better crop-growing, improved livestock breeding, and new farm equipment. The result – more and more was produced by fewer and fewer people. Farms got bigger and often stopped growing food. Instead they turned to crops like cotton, which were needed as raw materials in **textile** factories.

So where did all the out-of-work farming families go? To the cities.

Where did they find work? In factories, mills, and mines. Starting in the 1700s, people moved to cities by the thousands.

Metal workers in a ship-building foundry around 1900.

Chapter 5

More Changes

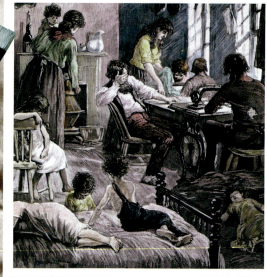

The Industrial Revolution took both workers and work out of the home and moved them into the factory. Cities were busy, noisy, smelly, and polluted. Many workers lived in cramped, dirty houses. They barely made enough money to survive. Men, women, and even children all worked long hours in difficult, often dangerous, conditions.

Smokestacks in Pittsburgh, Pennsylvania, in the 1890s.

Industrial Cities

Whole cities were built around single industries. Here are some examples:

Manchester, England, had cotton and textiles

Pittsburgh, Pennsylvania, had steel

Glasgow, Scotland, had shipbuilding

Where conditions were bad, workers began to demand improvement. Workers formed groups, called **unions**, so they could act together and bargain with employers and owners for more pay and safer working conditions. Often unions would go on **strike** to try to force an employer to meet their demands.

When workers go on strike, it can stop public transport systems or halt industry.

Chapter 6

A Job for Life

Once the idea of a "job" took hold, both employers and employees found that they liked stability.

Until only very recently, the late 1900s, many people spent their whole working lives with one business or one company. They learned a trade, such as welding or carpentry, then spent decades using what they'd learned.

In some places, a single industry, like mining or manufacturing, dominated a town. In these towns, grandfathers, fathers and sons often spent their whole lives working for one company.

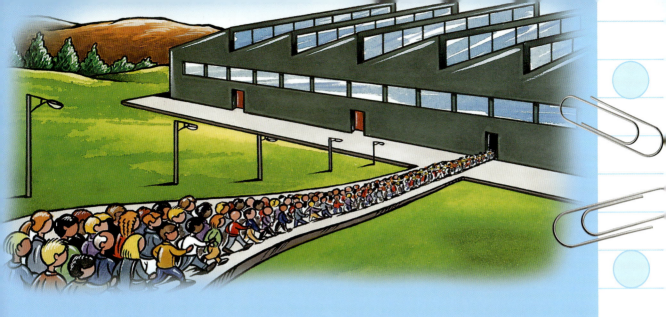

The companies encouraged loyalty. Some provided housing and health care. Most contributed towards the workers' **pensions.** Often there was a sense that the company would take care of you.

Workers punch into the time clock before they start work.

Chapter 7

Women and Work

By the early 1900s, the work that women did was very different from that of men. Men usually worked in manufacturing jobs and did professional work (like doctors and lawyers). Women mostly had clerical jobs (typing and filing), lower-paid factory positions, or worked as cleaners.

World War II changed all that. From 1939–45, as millions of men signed up to serve in the military, there was a shortage of workers. Women stepped into jobs that only men had done, such as welding and building ships.

The world of work had changed forever. Women enjoyed the independence, the money, and the chance to learn new skills.

Chapter 8

Information Revolution

Just as women were taking on wartime jobs, the seeds for the next revolution were being planted. Electronic computers appeared during the war. Over the next half century, as they became smaller and more powerful, they quickly spread to every corner of modern life.

Computers sparked the Information Revolution. It changed how we store and access information, how we communicate, and how we work.

If you wanted to draw the plans for the inside of a large building, it used to take a group of skilled draftsman two months to do the job. Software now means one person can do it in two days.

Chapter 9

The Amazing Disappearing Distance

In the 1800s, the railroad changed transportation. Never before had so many people traveled so far, so quickly and so often. The railway, more than any other means of transport before it (including ships), changed the way people thought about distance.

The Information Revolution is doing something similar today. But this time, distance is disappearing. Using a phone or a computer, you can reach anyone in the world, whenever you want. Cars can only transport us to limited places, but the internet can take us all around the globe.

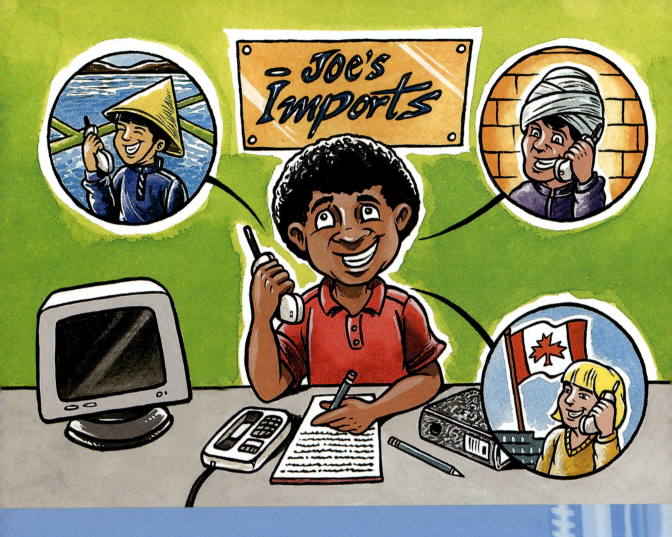

"Electronic commerce," known as **e-commerce** or e-business, means doing business using the internet. This means that no matter how small your business, you can work from anywhere. Now your customers can be from around the world. In this way, many companies have become global businesses, meaning they deal with people all over the world.

Chapter 10

What will Work Life be Like?

By the time you start working, the world will again be different. A job for life is already becoming a thing of the past. During one's lifetime, working for more than one or two companies and experiencing more than one type of job is becoming more common.

Over the years it is likely you'll work a series of jobs or work in contract (temporary) positions to gain skills and experience. You might work overseas for a while, and you might wait longer between jobs to get the right one. Perhaps you'll have more than one career – for example, a lawyer might become a writer, then turn to film making.

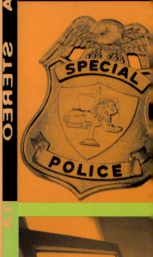

You might work full-time or more than one job that's part-time.

Your job may be something that hasn't been thought of yet. Sure, we'll still need jobs that are around now – chefs, mechanics, teachers, childcare workers, and so on. The Information Revolution has really only just started, so expect new jobs to keep springing up.

Remember, you can always start your own business and be the one who creates jobs for other people.

Glossary

Agricultural Revolution (also called Agrarian Revolution) a time during the 1700s and 1800s that saw major changes to farming practices, including more crops, better livestock breeding, and new farm equipment

cottage industry a system of working and making things at home. Merchants provided the raw materials, the workers created the products, then merchants collected them and paid workers part of the price they received for selling the products. Common products were cloth and clothing.

e-commerce short for electronic commerce, or business conducted electronically. Typically this means using the internet to buy goods online, or using internet banking.

Industrial Revolution a time during the 1700s and 1800s that saw the rise of mass-produced goods made by machines in factories

pensions money paid to workers upon retirement or disability

strike workers refusing to work to pressure their employer into meeting their demands

technology tools, knowledge, and inventions that help people do things

textile a cloth or fabric

unions organizations of workers, usually from the same industry, dedicated to improving the working conditions faced by those workers.